KAIRO -

MYSTICAL

KALEIDOSCOPE

by

Adenike Jones

Conscious Dreams
PUBLISHING

Kairo's Mystical Kaleidoscope

Copyright © 2022: Adenike Jones

First Printed in United Kingdom 2022

Published by Conscious Dreams Publishing

www.consciousdreamspublishing.com
@consciousdreamspublishing

Edited by Elise Abram and Daniella Blechner

Typeset by Oksana Kosovan

Cover Design by Jason Lee

ISBN: 978-1-915522-06-1

DEDICATION

For Linda

CONTENTS

CHAPTER 1

SCHOOL'S OUT

LAUGHTER SPILLED FROM THE CLASSROOM as the end-of-day bell rang to signal home time. It was Friday, the last day of the school week. In fact, it was the last school day for a couple of weeks as half-term was approaching. Kairo gathered his things and joined the line of children ready to follow their teacher to the playground to meet their parents. He glanced across to Tommy and his group of friends nervously. They were sniggering and pointing at him as they always did. They often teased and tormented him. It was, in fact, Tommy who had started the nickname of 'Kaleidoscope Kairo' that had quickly spread about the school.

'Hey, how was your day, son?' asked his mother as she greeted him and playfully tousled his tight, curly afro.

'It was okay, I guess,' Kairo replied, disappointed. 'They were laughing at me again.'

'Ah, don't you worry about that, son. Remember what we always tell you?'

'Yes, Mummy: I can be anything I want,' he replied, somewhat defiantly.

'That's right! Now, let's go home. Grandad is waiting to see you.'

✿✿✿

Home was No 2 Carey Walk, a short ten-minute drive from the school, where Kairo lived with his parents and older sister Eyabo, who spent most of her time on the phone, face-timing her friends. They were the very same friends she had probably already spent most of the day with. Kairo often wondered what more they could possibly have to talk about. It didn't really bother him because he was usually preoccupied with his own interests and spent his time mainly reading books about astronauts and space. If he wasn't doing that, he was spending time with his grandad.

Kairo loved it when his grandad visited. He would sit and talk with him for hours, listening to his stories from the past, but most importantly, he loved his grandad's enthusiasm when he spoke of his dream of becoming an astronaut. In fact, it was all Kairo ever wanted to talk about.

✩✩✩

As his mother parked the car on the driveway in front of No 2, Kairo quickly gathered his most prized possession, which he carried with him every single day, everywhere he went, and even took it to bed: his treasured kaleidoscope. He didn't care much for his school bag, which he'd casually thrown across the backseat.

Kairo was just nine-years-old. He was a sweet, carefree little boy. His skin tone was much fairer than that of his African parents—he had a kind of golden glow to his skin—he was always pleasant and cheerful. He had big brown eyes with long dark eyelashes and a bright, infectious smile that exposed his relatively new big front teeth.

He could practically feel his face light up when he saw his grandad peering through the window.

He quickly unbuckled his seat belt and hopped out of the car as his mummy held the door open for him. Without looking back, he raced up to the front door of the house, waving excitedly to Grandad, still clenching firmly onto his kaleidoscope all the while. It was as though it was a permanent extension of his arm.

'Ah, *omokunrin*!' Grandad said proudly—he often spoke in his native Nigerian language. Kairo had come to understand that the meaning of omokunrin was boy, and that was how Grandad often addressed him affectionately. 'My favourite boy—how was school?' he continued in English, although he still had a strong Nigerian accent attached to it. Kairo was quite aware that every boy was grandad's 'favourite boy.' It made him chuckle every time.

'Hi, Grandad,' he responded. 'School was fine, I guess,' he continued as he climbed effortlessly into his lap.

'Ah, I see you have your kaleidoscope—what a surprise.' He laughed out loud. He knew it was Kairo's pride and joy. He also knew he was in for another storytelling session.

Kairo laughed along, well aware that Grandad was the one person who would entertain stories of his kaleidoscope.

See, this wasn't just any kaleidoscope. This one was special. It was not like any other kaleidoscope that would normally project shapes and colours through mirrored glass when you peeked into it. There was a whole lot more to this one. This one had an extra slide attached to it, which, when rotated would act exactly like a telescope and enable him to see far away objects.

Kairo had been in possession of this most valuable toy since the age of five. He had become so attached to it that his parents and the headteacher at his school had come to an agreement that he could take it to his classes, assemblies, and school plays as long as it did not interfere with his schoolwork. The kaleidoscope was unique; it was special, this multi-coloured, circular tube that spun at one end, creating images whilst looking through a small hole at the other end. It was his absolute treasure because every time he looked through the small hole, and spun the extra slide, he saw only images of outer space.

Kairo had dreamt of becoming an astronaut since he was as young as two. He loved everything related to outer space and talked about nothing else, especially to his grandad, who would always listen enthusiastically and encourage him to never give up on his dream.

Many of the school kids often laughed at his space stories, but they had come to accept that Kairo and his toy were inseparable.

THE FANTASTIC FOUR

WEEKENDS WERE OFTEN A BUSY time in the household. Usually, a number of family members—aunties, uncles, and cousins—would gather to cook, talk, laugh, and play games. This weekend was no exception. Grandad had explained that three of Kairo's cousins and their parents would be shortly arriving to stay for the weekend. They were to have a day out the next day, but Kairo thought nothing of it as it wasn't out of the ordinary for the family to have a day out.

A short while later came the first knock at the door. It was his auntie and cousin of the same age, Isaac. They were greeted by the adults and ushered into the lounge. Isaac headed directly towards Kairo, who was pleased to see him. Isaac stood just a few inches taller than Kairo. He was dark-skinned with equally dark coloured eyes and hair. Isaac was an excitable boy, known to family as the inquisitive one as he was always asking questions; he was a very clever boy.

The boys exchanged their hellos and set immediately off towards Kairo's bedroom to see what they could play.

It wasn't much longer before his two other cousins arrived together with their families. They, too, joined Isaac and Kairo upstairs.

Lutae was the eldest of the four cousins at twelve years old. He stood very tall for his age, though the other children would tease him and say his tight, curly 'high top' afro made him seem taller than he was. He had a slender build and was always a charming young boy with a matter-of fact-attitude. He was the sensible one.

Then, there was Nai-emah — or Nai, as everyone called her — the only girl of the four. Nai was eleven-years-old and taller than Kairo, but she had not yet caught up to Lutae's height. She had the darkest skin tone of them all, as well as the prettiest smile. Nai was the tomboy of the group, often taking part in the boys' antics. She was tough in nature and wore her hair in cornrows, but she remained the sweetest character of them all.

The four were excited to see each other as they always had hours of fun when they stayed together.

After what seemed like hours of playing and laughing, the children were bathed, and they donned their pyjamas before Kairo's mum instructed them to go to bed. 'We have a busy day tomorrow,' she beamed, glancing over at Kairo.

'Where are we going?' he asked.

'You will see tomorrow, so get plenty of rest. Goodnight,' she replied. She pulled the door shut behind her, and the room fell into darkness.

CHAPTER 3

A DAY TRIP TO REMEMBER

THE BRIGHTNESS OF THE SUNSHINE peeking through the gap in the curtains shone directly into Kairo's face, waking him, and he jumped up excitedly. 'Get up, get up—we need to get ready for the trip!'

The other children sprung up out of bed just as excitedly, but Kairo was the first to rush downstairs, pounding against the carpeted steps, sounding like a herd of animals.

Grandad was already up, sitting in his usual spot. 'Ah, good morning. I take it you are up so early for your visit to the Space Museum?' He chuckled.

Kairo gasped. 'The Space Museum?' He stared at Grandad, waiting for confirmation of what he had just heard.

'Oh, dear—it seems I might have let the cat out of the bag,' he replied sheepishly, glancing across to the adults who had congregated in the kitchen.

'That's right,' interrupted Kairo's mum, rolling her eyes towards Grandad before looking over to him. 'We are all taking a day trip to The National Space Centre, space museum. I know you have wanted to visit it for a long time, so we arranged a family day out as a surprise. What do you think?'

'What do I think? Whoooa! The Space Museum! Yeah! I can't wait!'

The three other children had made their way down by then. 'Good morning,' they announced in unison, each with beaming smiles on their faces. They had heard the plans for the day and giggled as they watched Kairo, who was unable to contain his excitement. Eyabo, on the other hand, remained her in room. She knew of the plans for today's trip and had absolutely no interest in joining them. It was agreed she would stay at home with grandad.

✵✵✵

Everyone ate breakfast, washed, and dressed in no time. It seemed to be the speediest the children had ever managed to get ready.

They each donned their bright, shiny, silver spacesuits, which they had often played in before to entertain Kairo and his astronaut fantasy.

The journey to the Space Museum didn't take very long, but to Kairo, it felt like a lifetime. Upon approaching the building, he stared, feeling his eyes go wide with bewilderment at the size of the huge building standing before him.

The children speedily approached the secured entrance, and the parents followed on behind.

The place was bustling with people, families, groups of tourists, college students, and the general public.

'Wow, what amazing costumes!' said a tall, slim, fair-haired man approaching them. 'Good morning.' He introduced himself to everyone: 'I am your tour guide for today. My name is Steven.' He flashed a badge with his picture on it that he wore around his neck.

'I will be showing you around the Space Museum and answering any questions you may have.' He smiled welcomingly.

Kairo pushed towards the front of the group, and Isaac, Lutae, and Nai joined him. They looked fantastic in their spacesuits, which shimmered in the many bright lights in the entrance hall. Each of them had a backpack attached to a tube that led to their glass-fronted helmets. Isaac, Nai, and Lutae all carried their helmets under their arms. Kairo, on the other hand, wore his proudly in full spaceman mode. The visor had been left up so he could hear what was being said, but of course, he had that extra piece of equipment with him: his kaleidoscope.

'Can we see the spacecraft now?' he asked excitedly.

'Slow down, son. We will get to see everything in good time. We have all day.' Mum laughed.

Steven also laughed. 'Okay, let's get started,' he said, gesturing for the group to follow him. He walked and talked as they followed alongside him, marvelling at the information and displays they saw.

Finally, there it was: the moment for which Kairo had been so excitedly and impatiently waiting. There, before him, surrounded by a barrier of thick rope attached to black poles, all evenly spaced apart: the space shuttle formerly known as *Explorer.*

Kairo gasped. He stared. He froze on the spot.

'Whoa!' exclaimed Isaac, just as amazed as Kairo at the sight in front of him.

Nai and Lutae followed suit.

The parents searched around in their bags for cameras with which to take photographs of the gigantic structure. They, too, were in awe of the huge white aircraft with wings that looked as wide as the space shuttle was long; the large, black engines sitting on the back end of the craft; the blacked-out window at the front where the astronauts would sit; and the landing wheels, which looked surprisingly small for such a big machine. It was awesome!

Kairo turned to Steven. 'Can we go closer?'

'No, no, this is as close as we get. It's the most treasured piece of machinery here in the museum.'

Steven continued to inform the group of the story of the space shuttle, but at that point, neither Kairo nor the other children were listening. They were all busy sharing their observations with each other, pointing and running around the ropes, trying to see it from different angles, with Kairo clutching tightly to his kaleidoscope the whole time.

Steven gently urged the family to continue on with the tour, but at that moment, a security alarm sounded a loud, intermittent blaring noise. Steven instructed the group to evacuate the premises, signalling the direction in which they should proceed. People were startled, and they began to panic, wondering what was happening.

CHAPTER 4

LET THE ADVENTURE BEGIN!

AN ANNOUNCEMENT CAME OVER THE Tannoy, but Kairo and the others were having so much fun, snooping and peering at the space shuttle, that they didn't hear what was said. They were too busy running around the ropes trying to get the best possible view of this amazing structure.

The four children had hatched a plan to dare to board the spacecraft. They were having so much fun, they were oblivious as to what was happening around them.

They all entered through the rear door of the spacecraft without being stopped. Once inside, it was silent and cold.

Kairo was absolutely in his element. His dream had come true—he was on board the *Explorer*! He couldn't believe it. The others seemed just as excited as they surveyed the immensity of the aircraft.

Kairo headed immediately for the cockpit and took his place in the huge white leather seat, which made him feel so much smaller than he actually was. He gazed in awe at the machinery around him and the endless number of buttons, levers, and lights, struck by the sheer size of it. Ahead of him were the dark glass window screens.

'Quick, guys—take your seats. We're about to take off!' he yelled at the others. At the same time, he placed his kaleidoscope over his right eye whilst squinting with his left and peered through the hole. 'Quick! Buckle up! We're going into space. I can see!'

They rolled their eyes and glanced slyly at each other with smirks on their faces, but they did exactly as instructed, entertaining him by sitting in the seats on each side of the aircraft.

'Strap in,' he called, not taking his glance away from the kaleidoscope.

'Kairo, that's enough. We'd better get back before they realise we have gone,' said Lutae.

'No! Stay seated. We are about to take off!'

'Oh, he's seeing things through his mysterious kaleidoscope again,' said Isaac.

The other children laughed out loud.

'Come on—let's go,' said Lutae as he began to unbuckle his seatbelt.

29

Just then, the whole aircraft shuddered. The children felt a huge bolt from the rear, like something even bigger than the spaceship itself had kicked it from behind. They jolted forwards and backwards. The noise was intense, rowdy and quite scary. The engines began to accelerate, roaring and rumbling.

Startled and wide-eyed, they looked at each other.

'What was that?' Lutae shouted.

'I told you to sit down and buckle up. The spaceship is launching!' Kairo responded.

'Kairo, stop messing around. We have to go, now. Come on before we get into trouble,' continued Lutae

'Look!' Kairo said. He turned towards them and held out the kaleidoscope. 'See for yourself if you don't believe me.'

Nai took it from his grasp with a sigh. 'Give that to me,' she said, no doubt in an effort to humour him. She put the kaleidoscope to her right eye and squinted with her left just as Kairo had, spun the slide and she let out an almighty gasp. 'Oh, my goodness—it's true! Look!' She passed it across to Isaac as if it was something dirty she should never have touched, and she stared at him intently, waiting for his reaction.

Isaac took hold of it firmly, 'You do realise this is not a telescope, it's a kaleidoscope, don't you?' he stated, focusing solely on Kairo. 'What are you expecting me to see?' he continued.

Unwillingly, he took a look. He gulped.

'This can't be right. What's happening?' Isaac asked confused and bewildered.

'Do you believe me now? I told you. Now, sit down and strap in!' Kairo ordered. He wasn't fazed. He was in control. He was in his domain. This was his all-time dream come true. He was going to space, he was taking his 'crew' with him, and he loved it.

They all sat silently, stunned, unsure of what was about to occur. They were all scared, but nobody voiced it. They just sat, held on tightly to the bottom of their seats, and watched as Kairo took control.

With one hand holding his kaleidoscope to his face and the other hand on the control deck, he was ready. He was filled with excitement that he could tell wasn't shared with the other children. 'Hold on tight!' he shouted, and with that came the loudest roar he had ever heard.

They all screamed, and the aircraft shuddered again, this time continuously, and it got more and more vigorous; the noise was deafening.

Nai put her hands over her ears, clenched her knees together, and hung her head low.

Isaac held tightly onto his seat and never took his wide eyes off Kairo.

Lutae stared ahead of him, looking as if he could not quite believe what he was experiencing. 'We have to get out of here!' he eventually shouted.

'Too late for that.' Kairo laughed. 'We're on our way!'

Suddenly, they felt the spacecraft begin to lift off the ground. The noise intensified, the speed quickened and, within seconds, they were swiftly catapulted through the roof of the Space Museum. It was all so instantaneous, nobody spoke.

After a few minutes, the acceleration lessoned. They began cruising upwards. It was quieter.

Still clutching his toy to his face, Kairo whooped: 'Whoooooo-hoooooo! We are going into space!' He laughed loudly and fearlessly. He was in charge. He was flying the thing. 'I'm an astronaut. I'm an astronaut,' he exclaimed repeatedly.

'Cabin crew,' Kairo announced, 'we are now cruising at 34,000 feet.'

'This is actually happening. I can't believe it!' Isaac said.

'Is this some kind of a joke? How can this be happening?' Nai said quietly. Slowly, she unbuckled her seat belt. She soon found herself drifting around in the air. She gasped; the others gasped, too. They unbuckled themselves to experience the same weightlessness. It was then their fears turned into happiness, and their tears turned to laughter. They were floating. This was awesome.

Things that weren't attached floated randomly around them. They also spun around, laughing in amazement. Kairo wanted to join in the fun, so he passed his kaleidoscope to Lutae, urging him to look inside. He nodded his head to tell him it was okay to look through the scope. 'Look inside,' he said, 'we are in space.'

Lutae took the kaleidoscope and looked tentatively through the hole. 'Oh, my goodness… it's amazing. I can see stars. It's dark, yet it's so clear. What is happening?' He passed it to Isaac, who had the same reaction.

By then, likely dispelled of her fears, Nai said she wanted to take a look. Her jaw dropped when she brought it to her eye. She noticed how the sky appeared dark and was not the blue colour she was used to seeing. It was speckled with tiny white dots that she knew to be stars.

'Wow! This is the best day ever.'

Kairo Interrupted. 'And that's the power of my Kaleidoscope!' he said proudly. 'If you look out of the windows all you will see is pitch black, but if you use *MY* kaleidoscope and its special lens changing abilities, it lets you see the stars and much, much more. Who needs a telescope!'

They all laughed together as they spun around and travelled upside-down the length and breadth of the spaceship. 'Our hero, Kaleidoscope Kairo!' someone said.

One by one, they slowly took their seats again.

Chapter 5

COMMAND PILOT

'We're all astronauts!' Kairo laughed. 'Let me introduce myself: I am your command pilot, Kaleidoscope Kairo.'

'I am your trusty co-pilot, Lutae.'

'My name is Isaac, and I am your commander.'

'Nai,' she said, standing tall and proud, 'I am your back-up, Commander.' They saluted each other and burst into fits of laughter. Regardless of anything, they were the crew of the spaceship *Explorer*, two thousand and twenty!

All of a sudden, the *Explorer* shuddered and spluttered, startling them. Kairo quickly took his seat in the cockpit.

Lutae followed and took the second chair beside him. 'What's happening?' he asked.

Kairo grabbed his scope and proceeded to take a look without answering. 'We're landing! We're landing! Fasten your seatbelts. We're landing.'

'What do you mean, we're landing? Landing where? Landing on what?' Isaac persisted. He was nervous. Kairo could tell he was not sure what was going on or what to expect.

'Don't be so ridiculous.' Lutae chuckled. 'We can't land this thing. We're in space, remember?'

Kairo tossed his kaleidoscope across to him, landing it in his lap. 'Take a look if you don't believe me.' He continued to take command as though it was something he had done before.

Looking shocked, Isaac stared up at him as he dished out the orders.

'Helmets locked? Check. Oxygen supply connected? Check. Visor secure? Check. Crew, prepare for landing,' he continued, flipping switches, pressing buttons, and acting as the title of command pilot he had given himself.

The others followed suit, not questioning anything anymore. Within minutes, they were geared up in their spacesuits and ready to land.

The craft hovered in one spot above what looked like a planet beneath before it began to descend, seeming to fall silently compared to the roaring sounds earlier.

The children all focused on Kairo, awaiting his instructions. Then, with a loud crunch, the spaceship made contact.

Nai clutched her seat tightly once more.

'Let's go,' Kairo said.

'Wait—we can't go out there!' Lutae shouted.

'Of course, we can. Are you kidding me? We have flown the *Explorer*, landed the *Explorer*, and now we have to go and explore!' He laughed.

'We don't know what's out there.' Nai said.

'I'm scared,' Isaac interjected.

'I'm not sure about this, Kairo. I think we should go back. Everyone will be looking for us,' Nai said.

'No, we can't come this far and not see what's out there. We're astronauts, remember, team twenty-twenty? Come on,' Kairo insisted, and he led his crew to the bolted door.

'I wish Grandad was here to see this. He would love it,' Kairo announced.

Dust spat out from beneath his heavy, booted foot as he stepped cautiously forward. He looked around. It was dark, but at the same time, oddly bright. He continued to pace slowly forward, his feet lifting with each step as though in slow motion.

He turned and signalled to the others who had remained on the spacecraft and were watching him. He gestured for them to join him. Nobody moved. He hastily made his way back to the ship.

'Guys, you have to come and see this. I can't believe it! We've landed on the moon!' Kairo told them excitedly.

'You want us to go out there?' asked Lutae.

'No way. Uh-uh. I'm not going out there, and neither should you two,' said Isaac, directing his glance towards Nai and Lutae. 'We need to get out of here. Don't encourage him anymore,' he continued.

'Come onnn!' Kairo insisted. 'Didn't you hear me? We are on the moon! There's nothing to be scared of. We *have* to explore!'

'Oh, well,' Nai whispered angrily under her breath. 'I guess if the command pilot says so...'

They all dismounted the aircraft together.

Nai watched as the others explored, praying it wouldn't take too long for them to satisfy their curiosity so they could all return as quickly as possible to the spacecraft.

'Look at the size of these craters—they're huge,' Kairo shouted at them.

'What's a crater?' Isaac asked.

'It's what happens when asteroids and meteorites hit the lunar surface. On the surface of the moon there are thousands of craters.'

'No way,' said Lutae. 'Are you telling me we landed on the moon?' Kairo didn't need to answer him. He was sure his excitement and smile wide enough to make his cheeks ache said that they had, indeed, landed on the moon. They were actually standing on the surface of the moon.

They each beamed with joy. Nai stayed close to the others, not really participating, too stubborn to admit that it looked like fun.

Without warning, a massive rock-like object landed with a huge thud by the side of the craft. Fragments of rock scattered all around. Large and small rocks pelted down, blanketing the moon's surface. They all jumped and screamed at the same time. Kairo, looking towards the others, yelled at the top of his voice. 'Run! It's a meteor shower. Get back on the spaceship! Run!'

Isaac and Lutae didn't even look back, likely having sensed the fear in Kairo's voice. They ran as fast as they could, which in that kind of atmosphere and in those spacesuits proved to be quite a struggle. Their movements were much slower than they need be. With each stride, they bounced off the surface and back. They pressed on—nothing was going to stop them.

As Kairo lagged behind the others, he could see Lutae grab Nai's arm and pull her along with him. They had both managed to get ahead of Isaac.

The rocks continued to pelt down, hundreds of them, and at a speed that filled them with fear. As Lutae and Nai approached the spacecraft, a huge meteor plummeted and collided with the moon's surface. It was so powerful it rattled the steps, throwing them off their feet.

Nai groaned as she clambered back upright.

Isaac was close. He was almost caught up with Nai and Lutae. They dodged large and small rocks, running in zigzags, trying their hardest not to be struck.

Lutae was becoming hot in his helmet and suit and was breathing frantically, he made it up the steps and looked back to see if the others were close by.

Isaac was not far behind running, clumsily towards them.

'Hurry Isaac. You're almost here!' shouted Lutae.

He reached the steps, looking exhausted and frightened. He climbed onto the craft.

'Kairo!' Isaac he cried out. 'Kairo!'

Kairo could hear the calls from Isaac, although he was not within his sight.

'Kairo!' Lutae continued.

'I'm here,' a voice shouted from the near distance.

By now there was surface dust flying everywhere and it was getting darker by the minute.

'Run!' Lutae said upon spotting him. 'We have to get out of here. Hurry!'

'We can't leave. I dropped my kaleidoscope. I can't see it,' Kairo replied, practically hysterical.

'You have to come back. You're going to get hurt. Hurry.'

'I can't leave my kaleidoscope.' Kairo was on his knees, scrambling desperately around. He could hardly see his own gloved hand for the amount of dust. The rocks were relentless, smashing one after the other into the surface, narrowly missing him. He was so focused on finding his kaleidoscope that he became fearless to what was happening around him. He would not leave without it.

Kairo could hear Lutae order the other children to stay put on the aircraft and away from the door. He could also hear them voicing their objections.

'Kairo—where are you?' Lutae shouted.

Kairo could just about make out the figure heading towards him.

'Lutae!' he yelled, waving his hands above his head to catch Lutae's attention. 'I'm over here!'

Lutae spotted him crouched on his knees, arms waving in the air.

'Kairo, we have to get back right now!' he ordered. Not in the least bit entertained by this whole episode.

'My Kaleidoscope, can you see it? I can't find it. I dropped it when we were running, and now I can't find it. We can't get home without it. Please, help me.' Kairo pleaded.

'Okay. It's okay. We will find it, but we have to hurry—it's too dangerous out here,' said Lutae, resignedly.

The combination of flying dust on the surface and trying to see clearly was proving very hard; Kairo could barely make out Lutae who was now kneeling. The only thing they could rely on was to feel around on the ground, in the craters and behind the rocks, but even that was a task because their gloves were so thick.

Kairo was becoming exhausted—dodging the meteors and searching desperately for his kaleidoscope were taking their toll. He was becoming despondent. Thoughts whizzed around in his head. What if he never found it? What if they were are stuck there forever? How would they survive?

'It's here! I found it. It's here!' Lutae shouted across to him.

He had indeed finally located the kaleidoscope. He had felt one end of it protruding from behind a fallen rock, the other end had nestled into the sand like surface. He pulled it out, not even taking a second to check for damage.

'Thank the Lord!' Kairo exclaimed, reaching out his hand. 'Let me see.'

'No, I will hold it. We need to get back to the spaceship right now!'

'I need—'

'Right now!' Lutae repeated firmly. Kairo knew it was because he didn't want to waste any more time. Like Kairo, Lutae was probably tired, frustrated, and wanted nothing more than to be home.

Neither uttered another word as they fought their way back, safely to the *Explorer*.

Shaken and upset, they prepared to make the journey back.

'That was scary,' Isaac piped up. 'I'm not going to pretend it wasn't.'

'We're not out of the woods yet. We still have to get this thing off the ground,' Lutae said, looking over at Kairo.

'Don't worry. You're back in safe hands.' Kairo smiled as he wiped the dust from his kaleidoscope, brought it close to his ear, shook it gently, just to make sure nothing was broken. He also checked through the eyepiece to be sure he could see clearly.

'All correct and present,' he affirmed to the others.

Nai rolled her eyes. 'Can we just go already?'

They strapped themselves in. The noise outside was still powerful. Clanging metal sounded each time a rock pelted the spaceship.

The trembling of the *Explorer* began again as the engines started up.

'Yeah, I think Nai is right. Let's go!' Issac agreed.

Kairo realized, come to think of it, that they had all deemed Kairo their leader, and they wanted his approval before any decisions were made. Kairo was comfortable with his position of authority. After all, he had been telling them for a very long time that his kaleidoscope was like no other, and now they believed him at last.

'Sit tight!' he ordered. He looked through his precious scope and remained silent as Lutae watched on. He took a moment to glance over at Lutae, still silent.

✧✧✧

Back on planet Earth, fire engines had arrived at the museum and were stationed at the entrance and side of the building. Hundreds of people gathered at the fire assembly point at the museum. The siren continued to sound in the distance, and the hustle and bustle of visitors and their families continued.

`The fire marshals stood near the front of the crowd in illuminous green, high visual jackets, communicating with each other over walkie-talkies.

Kairo's mum, along with her team, had managed to make their way to the front of the roped barriers that had been put into place so she could hear what was being said amongst the fire marshals. 'Excuse me? Excuse me?' she called to the marshal standing to her left.

He glanced at her and made a hand signal with his index finger as if to say, 'One minute,' as he continued on his radio.

She stared across at him, waiting impatiently, not taking her eyes off of him, desperately trying to control her anxiety.

Eventually, he looked back at her and began towards her.

'The children...*our* children...we can't find them. We were separated. We can't find them. Please, help.' She spewed it all out in one go without taking a breath.

'Okay. Okay, madam, please, calm down.' He gestured as he patted her shoulder gently. 'How many children are missing?'

'Four. Three boys and one girl,' she informed him.

'One minute they were here, then the alarms went off and we were separated in the rush,'sShe continued. 'You have to help us find them.'

The marshal lifted the ropes and ushered Kairo's family, to stand aside whilst he made some enquiries.

He communicated via his radio for what, to Kairo's mum, felt like an hour but was probably only a matter of minutes, then he turned to her and said, 'Our officers have checked the building, ma'am, and they have no sightings of anyone left inside. They are, however, continuing to search.'

'But—'

'I would presume they are probably mixed in with the crowd. Don't worry—we will get you reunited,' he assured them.

'Ma'am, please, try to stay calm. All of our officers are looking for the four children.' He explained, as he noticed the worrying look on her face.

The family stood and clenched hands as they waited patiently for news of their children.

CHAPTER 6

HOMEWARD BOUND

BACK ON THE MOON, LOUD banging noises sounded against the craft like the sound of hailstones, only this time it sounded heavier, more intense.

'Let's get moving. I don't like this,' Isaac said.

'Everyone, hold on tight. This is going to be a bumpy ride. The meteors are everywhere,' Kairo instructed.

'Well, hurry up and use your stupid toy that got us here in the first place,' snapped Nai. She slumped back into her seat and sulked.

Both Kairo and Lutae ignored her. They were too busy scanning through the hundreds of levers and buttons in front of them.

'There must be something here that will help,' Lutae said.

'No! Don't press anything. My kaleidoscope got us here, and it will get us back.'

'Okay, okay.' Lutae threw both hands up to acknowledge he wasn't about to touch anything.

'Let me figure this out,' Kairo said. He took off his helmet and laid it on the floor in front of him.

What sounded like firecrackers were going off outside of the craft, along with swooshing noises, bangs, and clangs. They seemed to be getting louder and more frequent.

'Nai, it's okay. We will be home soon,' Kairo reassured her once he noticed the look of fear on her face. Not surprisingly, Kairo wasn't scared at all. He had encountered many missions such as this in his imagination as he played with his kaleidoscope, only this time it was for real.

It was surprising how the boys and Nai sat so patiently watching, waiting, and hoping that Kairo had a solution to get them out of there and quick. Kairo continued engaging himself, flicking switches, turning knobs—the very same one's he had ordered Lutae not to touch. He continued checking through the peek hole of his kaleidoscope from time to time, listening closely to the sounds as if he recognised them. He did all of this as if he were alone, but Nai's increasingly nervous fidgeting finally broke his concentration.

'It's getting louder!' she announced, unable to keep quiet any longer.

'Shush—I can't concentrate,' Kairo responded.

Lutae climbed up to the nearest cockpit window and looked out. 'We definitely need to start moving. It's getting worse out there. If we don't go now, we never will.' He didn't turn around. 'If these meteors hit the spaceship, we will be stuck here forever, and no one will know where to find us.'

'Okay, Assistant Commander Lutae, please return to your seat. Prepare to ascend,' Kairo ordered, unfazed by the panic in Lutae's voice.

Even with everything that was happening, he was still in his role of first commander, and the others didn't question it; they just played along. All they wanted was to get back home, and if that meant entertaining Kaleidoscope Kairo, then that's what they would have to do. They donned their helmets and followed his orders. Kairo took a long look through his kaleidoscope before laying it on his lap and taking a deep breath. 'Okay. This is it. Here we go!'

He fired up the engine. The craft shunted forward slightly. The engine roared louder. Isaac held on tightly. Nai clung to the base of her seat.

The spacecraft picked up the charge and lifted slightly off the ground. 'Hold on!' Kairo shouted without turning around. It hit the ground abruptly once more. Again, he attempted the same actions. It lifted again and swung from side-to-side. This sequence happened four or five more times before eventually, on the sixth attempt, the spaceship shot up with full force.

The crew jerked backwards and forwards as the huge machine took up speed. The engines roared loudly as they gained height. Kairo was pinned to his kaleidoscope, shouting instructions to Lutae to ensure they would dodge the many, many meteors firing around them.

'LEFT!' Kairo commanded, and the aircraft spun suddenly to the left, causing everyone to jolt forwards.

'Whoaaa,' screamed Isaac. Kairo could see that his piercing eyes were wide open.

'RIGHT! LEFT!' Kairo continued to shout orders, and Lutae tried to keep up with his demands.

The spaceship spun recklessly. Isaac's seatbelt suddenly unbuckled, ejecting him upwards. The loss of gravity within the aircraft caused him to float aimlessly around.

Lutae undid his belt and grabbed him while Nai watched, frozen to the spot.

Kairo dropped his kaleidoscope and helped Lutae secure Isaac back into his seat.

The *Explorer* spiralled out of control, and the children screamed for Kairo to take back control of his Kaleidoscope.

He obeyed, secretly elated that they believed him that his toy was different and magical. Kairo smiled to himself as he proudly took control of the situation.

It felt like a lifetime, but he eventually managed to manoeuvre away from danger, and they were now cruising at a safe altitude and heading back home.

'Gentlemen...and lady.' The first commander giggled. 'We will be arriving at our destination shortly.'

'Cool! We did it.' Lutae laughed.

'About time, too,' replied Nai.

'HA! You were scared,' pointed out Isaac.

With that, they all laughed so much they cried.

CHAPTER 7

GROUNDED

THE FOUR CHILDREN DISMOUNTED AND found themselves back at the space museum.

'That was some day out,' Kairo said. 'I can't wait to tell my grandad.'

'Hey, where is everyone?' Lutae asked.

It was only then that they all realised there was no one else in the museum, not their families, not the tour guides, not a single person. It was so quiet.

'How long have we been gone? The place is deserted,' Isaac said.

'My mum wouldn't have just left us here. Something must have happened,' Kairo said.

'Let's get to the exit. They must be waiting for us there,' said Lutae.

They walked in a pack. Kairo held onto his helmet with one hand and clenched his kaleidoscope in the other.

'Hey, stop there!' a voice called to them. Walking towards them was a tall, heavily-built security guard. 'Everyone has been searching for you. Where have you children been hiding all this time?' he asked.

'We went to the moon!' Kairo replied, beaming with excitement.

'Oh, is that right?' said the guard, smirking.

'That's right. Onboard the *Explorer* itself,' said Kairo proudly.

'Oh, I guess would that be the very same *Explorer* that mysteriously went missing, would it?' He laughed. 'Well, while you were off on the moon, your parents have been very worried about you, so I'll take you to them now and let you explain that to them.' He shook his head. 'Follow me.'

It was nightfall by then. Everyone who had been evacuated from the museum earlier that day had gone, all except for Kairo's mum, aunties and uncles. They had been allowed to sit in the foyer and wait for information concerning their missing children.

When the door flung open, and the security guard appeared, they all gasped at the sight of their children running towards them.

'Kairo, my boy—where have you been? We've been so worried about you! Are you okay?' His mum checked him over from head to toe to make sure he wasn't injured.

'I'm fine, Mum. You won't believe it—we went to space. We took the *Explorer* and went to the Moon, and—' Kairo replied breathlessly, excited to tell their story.

'Kairo,' she stopped him, 'this is not the time for one of your fantasy stories—do you know how worried we have been?'

'No, it's true. We—'

'Lutae, Isaac, Nai, are you all okay? Your parents have been frantic. Oh, my goodness, what a day this has been,' she continued, not taking further interest in Kairo's story.

'Is everything OK ma'am?' asked the security guard as he approached Kairo's mum.

'Oh yes, sir. Thank you very much for your help. They are all fine,' she said, nodding in reply. 'They tried to tell me a story about going to space,' she said, rolling her eyes.

'Ah yes. I heard that too,' he smiled. 'Let me escort you all to the exit.'

The family thanked the security guards, said their goodbyes and made their way home.

✩✩✩

The journey back home was silent upon Kairo's mum's insistence. She'd said she wasn't in the mood to hear any more stories about the moon. She was exhausted and quite angry with the children for not acknowledging the upset and worry they had caused the family. She drove in silence, occasionally mumbling to herself and shaking her head.

It was difficult for them to keep quiet for too long. They were still bursting with excitement at what they had experienced and wanted to shout about it. They sniggered and whispered in the back of the car, frequently checking the rear-view mirror to see if Kairo's mum was listening. It felt like the longest journey home.

Kairo, Lutae, Isaac, and Nai were collectively reprimanded for causing the family distress and warned of the dangers of not staying close to their parents when out and about.

'Those spacesuits went to their heads,' chuckled Kairo's mum. The adults were in agreement at least but the children just frowned.

'Went to the moon, they said,' she continued to mock.

'But it's true. We really did,' Lutae piped up.

'It's true. We're telling you the truth,' Nai added.

'Okay, okay...that's enough of that,' Kairo's mum responded with a straight face while shaking her head. 'Take yourselves upstairs and get out of those suits and wash up for dinner.'

As they made their way upstairs, Kairo glanced across the lounge to where his grandad was fast asleep in his chair. I bet Grandad wouldn't laugh at us. He would believe it's true, he thought to himself.

With all the adventures earlier that day, the children hadn't realised just how hungry they were—they had forgotten about eating altogether—so dinner went down like a treat.

'What happened to your kaleidoscope?' Grandad had woken and noticed that Kairo's pride and joy looked a little worse for the wear. He held his hand out to suggest he wanted to take a closer look.

'It looks as though you were throwing it around, my boy. You are usually so protective of it.' He studied the toy closely.

'No, Grandad, I dropped it. I dropped it on the moon's surface when we were trying to dodge the huge meteor shower!' he said excitedly, knowing Grandad would understand. He knew Grandad, of all people, would listen.

'Oh!' Grandad said, looking at him wide-eyed. 'The moon, eh?

'Come and tell me all about it,' he said, turning around to make his way back to his chair. He walked at a snail's pace with the aid of a walking stick.

That was it. He didn't need to be told twice. Kairo jumped off the dining room chair and was already waiting beside Grandad's chair for him.

'I used to be fast like that, son,' Grandad smiled.

An hour later, Kairo was still filling in Grandad on their great adventure. Isaac, Lutae, and Nai had joined them, sitting in a semi-circle in front of Grandad's chair, often adding their parts to the story. Grandad was fully engaged. He laughed, he gasped, he indulged them in telling more, just like Kairo knew he would.

There was a knock at the door.

Kairo's mum went to answer. 'Who could be knocking at this late hour?' She opened the door. 'Oh!' She took a step back as if surprised to see two uniformed men standing on the doorstep.

'Excuse me, ma'am. We apologise for calling so late in the day. My name is First Commander Adetunde Odunsi, and this,' he gestured to the man on his right, 'is Commander Matt Wilson. We are from the The National Space Centre—do you mind if we come in? We would like a minute of your time.'

'Errm...sure. Yes, come in. Errm...how can I help you?' she replied.

Kairo noticed his mum was somewhat nervous. No one had any idea as to why these uniformed men, one of which—who was tall, stocky, and dark-skinned with a Nigerian name and accent—Kairo recognised from the museum. The other was slightly shorter, fair-skinned, and had light-coloured, shaven hair. They both appeared very smart in their attire, but why did they need to speak to her?

'Please, don't look so worried.' Mr Odunsi smiled at her reassuringly.

Kairo's mum invited them to be seated. She introduced them to the family, who had stopped in their tracks when they'd noticed them enter the house.

The children leapt up to join the rest of the family, along with Granddad, whom Kairo was sure was equally as intrigued.

'We would like to bring to your attention to an incident that occurred today at the science museum. I believe you visited today as a family?' the first commander continued.

'Ah, yes. That's right,' Kairo's mum replied. 'We apologise for any disruption we may have caused. You see, there was a fire alarm, and we got separated from the children for quite a while, but everything turned out fine. The security guard found them after all. They had been hiding.' She carried on nervously. 'Although they told us another story about the going to the moon.' She rolled her eyes.

'Well, actually, ma'am, that's why we are here,' he interrupted. 'You see, today, something really quite strange happened at the museum, something neither myself nor my fellow astronauts have ever witnessed before.'

'Oh?' Kairo's mum frowned.

'Did you hear that? They're astronauts,' Kairo whispered to the others, unable to contain his excitement.

'Shh...listen,' Lutae responded.

'What exactly happened?' Kairo's mum asked, with a puzzled look on her face.

'Well, upon viewing the security video footage prior to and after the alarm sounding...' the officer clearing his throat, 'it would appear that four children, each wearing spacesuits, were seen boarding the *Explorer* spacecraft, the same four that were subsequently reported as missing.'

The children sat quietly and stared on.

Mr Wilson glanced over at them.

'Oh, yes…errm…' Kairo's mum still seemed a little unnerved.

'The thing is,' continued Mr Odunsi, 'the footage shows that for approximately thirty-five minutes, the *Explorer* disappeared. It later reappeared, and the same four children disembarked the aircraft.'

Kairo jumped to his feet, kaleidoscope in hand, and ran across to his mother. 'Mummy, I told you, and you didn't believe us. We went to the moon in the spaceship! Tell them,' Kairo instructed Nai, Issac and Lutae. 'Tell them we went to the moon. I was the first commander.

It was my kaleidoscope that got us there and back!' He was so excited he could hardly catch his breath.

The children joined in with equal enthusiasm. They all seemed to be screaming out the story at once.

'What is happening?' Kairo's mum asked. 'I don't understand.'

Grandad laughed out loud as he watched on, and Kario knew it was because he knew his boy was telling the truth.

The commanders invited them to come and tell their extraordinary story to members of the board before bidding them goodnight. Upon leaving, the first commander shook Kairo's hand and said, 'Good to meet you, young man. You are quite the astronaut. We can't wait to hear all about it.'

Kairo was stunned. He had called him an astronaut! He'd shaken his hand!

The children jumped for joy. In fact, the whole family jumped for joy.

☆☆☆

They sat up for hours that night, listening to the whole unbelievable adventure the children had been on.

CHAPTER 8

LESSONS LEARNED

A FEW DAYS LATER, THE children were known nationally. The newspapers printed their story, and the local radios interviewed them. They were hailed as local heroes. The *Explorer* had become the number one attraction in the whole of England, with visitors travelling from all over the world just to see the machine that had been pelleted by meteors and brought back to Earth by four incredible children.

✧✧✧

Sales of kaleidoscopes rocketed. With every child wanting one, the stores couldn't keep up with the demand, but everyone knew there was none other as special and unique as Kairo's.

His was known worldwide, but the biggest gift of all was a V.I.P invite to The National Space Centre, where he would get to meet inspiring astronauts. He was the happiest kid in the whole wide world.

His parents were so proud of him, especially Grandad, who, on this day, the first day back after the half-term break, insisted on escorting Kairo to school.

They were met with cheers and applause. The forecourt was filled with children, parents, and teachers, all of them wanting to catch a glance of him. There he stood, still the shy, reserved little boy, and still with his now even more precious belonging in his hand.

Grandad walked slowly across to a small group of boys as Kairo watched on puzzled. 'Which one of you is Tommy?' he asked.

'That's me...errm, sir. I am Tommy,' he replied, fidgeting and nervous.

Grandad greeted him with a smile. 'Tommy,' he said softly, 'let this be a lesson that you should never torment or make fun of another person's dreams,' he pointed across to Kairo, 'because he is proof that you can be whatever you want'.

'But' he continued, 'I want to let you know that thanks to you, the entire world now knows of the nickname Kaleidoscope Kairo!'

ABOUT THE AUTHOR

THIS IS THE SECOND INSTALMENT of children's fiction by Adenike Jones. She lives in Manchester UK, daughter to a Nigerian father and English mother. She is the author of children's book, *Renae's Magical Wellington Boots*.

Her inspiration for stories in children's fantasy, comes from her five grandchildren and watching them grow with a passion for reading. Her dream was always to write her own books and take young children on journeys that would ignite their imaginations.

Conscious Dreams
PUBLISHING

Transforming diverse writers
into successful published authors

www.consciousdreamspublishing.com

authors@consciousdreamspublishing.com

Let's connect

Lightning Source UK Ltd.
Milton Keynes UK
UKHW022013010922
408212UK00011B/89